THE FISH
AND HIS ...

D0537167

Illustrated by Rusty Fletcher

Adapted by Sarah Toast

ISBN: 0-7853-1923-9

PUBLICATIONS INTERNATIONAL, LTD.
Stories to Grow On is a trademark of Publications International, Ltd.

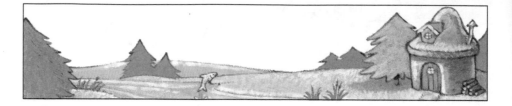

Once a poor fisherman and his wife lived in a little cottage near a river. Every day the fisherman went to the river and fished for their dinner.

One day the fisherman caught a magical fish in his net. It said, "Fisherman, I beg you to let me live. I am not really a fish, I am an enchanted prince. Please let me swim away."

The fisherman quickly agreed to let the fish go. "Say no more," said the fisherman. "I am quite willing to set free a fish that can talk!"

"For that, I will grant you a wish," said the fish. The fisherman said there was nothing he needed.

The fisherman let the fish go free. When he went home, his wife asked, "Husband, what have you caught for me to cook for our dinner?"

"I haven't brought anything home," he said. "I caught a big fish who said he was an enchanted prince, so I threw him back into the water."

"Oh dear!" she said. "You might at least have made a wish before you set him free!"

"What would I wish for?" asked her husband.

"Well, we certainly could use a nicer place to live. I'm sure that if you go back and ask the fish for a nicer house, he will gladly give it to you!"

The fisherman did not really think that they needed a nicer house, but he did as his wife asked.

The fisherman went to the river and called:
Princely fish that I set free,
Hear my words and come to me.

The fish soon appeared. The fisherman said, "My wife would like to make a wish after all."

"And what is her wish?" asked the fish.

"She doesn't want to live in a tiny cottage anymore," said the fisherman. "She would like to live in a nicer home."

"Go home to your wife," said the fish. "She already has her wish."

The fisherman hurried back home. There was his wife waving from the doorway of a nice new house.

The house was filled with everything the fisherman and his wife could possibly need. "Now we can be happy," the fisherman said.

But a few days later the wife said, "Husband, this house is too small. We need more space! Go back to the river and ask the fish for a castle!"

The fisherman wanted his wife to be happy. He returned to the river and called:

> *Princely fish that I set free,*
> *Hear my words and come to me.*

"Now what?" asked the fish.

"Alas, my wife wants to live in a castle," said the fisherman regretfully.

"Go home. She is already there," said the fish.

When the fisherman returned home, his wife waved to him from the balcony of a huge castle. Its rooms were full of golden furniture, and the tables were filled with wonderful things to eat.

"Isn't everything beautiful?" asked the wife. The fisherman agreed. He was sure that now they had everything they could ever possibly need.

But early the next morning the wife woke up frowning. She said, "Husband, we live in a castle, so we should be king and queen of all the land."

The fisherman didn't want that at all, but his wife insisted. The unhappy fisherman finally gave in and went back to the river.

Once again the fisherman called:
Princely fish that I set free,
Hear my words and come to me.

"What is it now?" asked the fish.

"I'm afraid my wife wants us to be king and queen," sighed the fisherman.

"Go home. She is already queen," said the fish.

Sure enough, when the fisherman arrived back at the castle, his wife was sitting on a high gold throne. "Now that you are queen," said the fisherman, "surely you will not want to wish for anything more."

"I'm not at all sure of that," said the queen. "I have a feeling there is something else we need."

That night the fisherman slept well, but his wife lay awake tossing and turning and wondering about what her next wish would be.

Just as the wife was about to fall asleep, the sun came up. Bright sunlight streamed in through the royal bedroom window. The wife sat up in bed.

"Husband!" she said. "I do not think the sun should be allowed to rise without my permission! Go tell the fish I want to have power over the rising and setting of the sun!"

"Wife," said the fisherman, "I think that is too much to ask!"

At this, the wife flew into a rage. "Go tell the fish to grant my wish!" she shouted.

Quaking with fear, the fisherman got dressed. He hurried out of the castle and headed toward the river. As he walked, strong winds began to blow and the river began to rage.

The fisherman stumbled to the riverbank. He could barely hear his own voice over the fierce wind as he called:

> *Princely fish that I set free,*
> *Hear my words and come to me.*

"What does your wife want now?" asked the fish as he rose up through the choppy waves.

"Oh, fish," said the fisherman fearfully, "she wants the power to make the sun rise and set."

"Go home to your wife," said the fish.

Suddenly, the wind stopped as quickly as it had started. The fisherman went home to find his wife in front of their humble cottage again.

"Husband," said the wife, "I am so sorry that I got carried away with greed. Each new and better thing just made me want more. But the more I got, the more unhappy I became."

"It's my fault, too," the fisherman said. "When you wanted more, I asked the fish for it." The fisherman kissed his wife, took his net, and went to the river. He gazed into the clear blue water as he fished.

That night he brought his wife a nice, plain fish for their dinner.

One to Grow On

Moderation

The fisherman and his wife learned a lot about moderation. Moderation means not having too much or too little of anything. Instead of being thankful for what she had, the fisherman's wife always wanted more.

Have you ever had too much of something? Like the fisherman and his wife, maybe you have learned that less can be better. Sometimes simple things can make us happier than all the castles and crowns in the world.